"Yuri Herrera's novels are like little lights in a vast
darkness. I want to see whatever he shows me."
Stephen Sparks, Green Apple Books, San Francisco, CA.

"This is as noir should be, written with all the grit and
grime of hard-boiled crime and all the literary merit we're
beginning to expect from Herrera. Before the end he'll
have you asking how, in the shadow of anonymity, do you
differentiate between the guilty and the innocent?"
Tom Harris, Mr B's Emporium, Bath.

"Both hysterical and bleak, *The Transmigration of Bodies*
builds an entire world in 100 pages. Herrera's ability to
express everything in so few words, his skill of merging
the argot of the streets with the poetry of life is unrivaled.
The world his characters inhabit is dangerous and urban,
like a postcard sent from the ends of the earth. Reading his
compact novels is both exhilarating and unforgettable."
Mark Haber, Brazos Bookstore, Houston, TX.

"A fabulous book full of low-life characters struggling to get by. It's
an everyday story of love, lust, disease and death. Indispensible."
Matthew Geden, Waterstones Cork, Ireland.

KINGDOM CONS

Yuri Herrera

Translated by
Lisa Dillman

SHEFFIELD – LONDON – NEW HAVEN

First published in English translation in 2017 by And Other Stories
Sheffield – London – New Haven
www.andotherstories.org

First published as *Trabajos del reino* in 2008
by Editorial Periférica, Madrid, Spain

ISBN: 978-1-908276-92-6
eBook ISBN: 978-1-908276-93-3

Editor: Tara Tobler; Typesetter: Tetragon, London; Typefaces: Linotype Swift
Neue and Verlag; Cover Design: Hannah Naughton. Printed and bound by the
CPI Group (UK) Ltd, Croydon, CRO 4YY.

A catalogue record for this book is available from the British Library.

This book was supported using public funding by Arts Council England.

Supported using public funding by

**ARTS COUNCIL
ENGLAND**

MIX
Paper | Supporting
responsible forestry
FSC FSC® C171272
www.fsc.org

KINGDOM CONS

He knew blood, and could see this man's was different. Could see it in the way he filled the space, with no urgency and an all-knowing air, as though made of finer threads. Other blood. The man took a seat at a table and his attendants fanned out in a semicircle behind him.

Lobo admired him in the waning light of day that filtered in through a small window on the wall. He had never had these people close, but was sure he'd seen this scene before. The respect this man and his companions inspired in him had been set out somewhere, the sudden sense of importance he got on finding himself so close. He recognized the way the man sat, the lofty look, the glimmer. Then he saw the jewels that graced him and knew: he was a King.

The one time Lobo had gone to the pictures he saw a movie with a man like this: strong, sumptuous, dominating the things of the world. He was a King, and around him everything became meaningful. Men gave their lives for him, women gave birth for him; he protected and bestowed, and in the kingdom, through his grace, each and every subject had a precise place. But those accompanying this King were more than vassals. This was his Court.

Lobo felt envy, the bad kind first and the good kind after, because suddenly he saw that this was the most important day of his life. Never before had he been near one of those who gave life meaning, made it all tally up. Never even had the hope. Ever since his parents had brought him here from who knows where and then abandoned him to his fate, life had been a counting off of days of dust and sun.

A voice thick with phlegm distracted his gaze from the King: a drunk, ordering him to sing. Lobo complied, effortlessly at first, still trembling with excitement; but soon, from the same, he sang like never before, pulling words out from inside as though pronouncing them for the first time, as though overcome by the ecstasy of having happened upon them. He felt the King's eyes on his back and the cantina fall silent; people put their dominoes facedown on tables to listen. He sang a song and the drunk demanded Another and then Another and Another and Another, and with each one Lobo sang more inspired, and the drunk got more drunk. At times he joined in, at times he spat into the sawdust and laughed with the old soak there with him. Finally he said Okay, and Lobo held out his hand. The drunk paid and Lobo saw it was short and held out his hand once more.

"That's it, songbird. What I got left is for one more shot. Just thank your saints you got that much."

Lobo was used to it. These things happened. And he was about to turn away in What Can You Do resignation, when he heard from behind:

"Pay the artist."

Lobo turned to see the King holding the drunk in his gaze. He said it calm. It was a simple order, but the man didn't know enough to stop.

"What artist?" he said. "Only thing I see here is this fool and I already paid him."

"Don't get smart, friend," the King's voice hardened. "Pay him and shut it."

The drunk got up and staggered to the King's table. His men went on alert, but the King sat unflustered. The drunk struggled to focus and then said:

"I know you. I heard what they say."

"That a fact? And what do they say?"

The drunk laughed. Clumsily scratched a cheek.

"Nah. Not your business I'm talking about, everybody knows that . . . Talking about the other."

And he laughed once more.

The King's face clouded. He tilted his head back, got up. Signaled his entourage to stay put. Approached the drunk and grabbed his chin. The man tried to twist free: no luck. The King put his lips to the drunk's ear and said:

"Actually, I don't think you heard a thing. You know why? Because dead men have very poor hearing."

The King put his gun to him as tho feeling the man's gut, and fired. A simple shot. Nonchalant. The drunk opened his eyes wide, tried to steady himself on a table, slipped and fell. The King turned to the boozer with him.

"You got something to say too?"

The man snatched his hat and fled, hands high in a Didn't See A Thing. The King bent over the corpse, rifled through a pocket, pulled out a wad of bills. He peeled off a few, handed them to Lobo, replaced the rest.

"Artist, take your due," he said.

Lobo took the bills without looking down. He was staring at the King, drinking him in. And kept watching as the King signaled his crew and they filed slowly out of the cantina. Lobo gazed at the swinging doors. And thought that from now on there was a new reason why calendars were senseless: no date meant a thing besides this one. Because finally he'd found his place in the world. And because he'd heard something about a secret, which he damn well wanted to keep.

Dust and sun. Silence. A sorry house where no one exchanged words. His parents a couple of strays who got lost in the same corner, nothing to say to each other. That was why the words started to pile up, first in Lobo's mouth and then in his hands. For him school was brief, a place where he sensed the harmony of letters, the rhythms that strung them together and split them apart. It was a private discovery, since he couldn't see the lines on the chalkboard clearly and the teacher took him for a fool, and he confined himself to the solitude of his notebook. And it was out of sheer passion that he mastered the ways of syllables and accents, before being ordered to earn his keep on the street, offering rhymes in exchange for pity, for coins.

The street was hostile territory, a muffled struggle whose rules made no sense; he managed to endure it by repeating sweet refrains in his head and inhabiting the world through its public words: posters, papers sold on street corners, signs. These were his antidote to chaos.

He'd stop on the sidewalk and run his eyes again and again over any random string of words to forget the fierce environs around him.

One day his father put the accordion in his hands. Coldly, as tho instructing him on how to unjam a door, he taught Lobo to combine the chord buttons on the left with the basses on the right, how the bellows trap and release air to shape the sounds.

"Now hold it good," he said, "This is your bread."

The next day his father went to the other side. They waited in vain. Then his mother crossed without so much as a promise of return. They left him the accordion so he could make his way in the cantinas, and it was there he learned that while boleros can get by with a sweet face, corridos require bravado and acting out the story as you sing. He also learned the following truths: Life is a matter of time and hardship. There is a God who says Deal with it, cause this is the way it is. And perhaps the most important: Steer clear of a man about to vomit.

He never took notice of the calendar. It seemed absurd because days were all alike: do the rounds of the tables, offer songs, hold out your hand, fill your pockets with change. Dates earned a name only when someone took pity on themselves or another by pulling out steel and shortening the wait. Or when Lobo discovered hairs cropping up or things getting bigger on his body at will. Or when pain hacksawed his skull and struck him down for hours at a time. Endings and eccentricities were the most notable way to order time. That was how he spent it.

That, and learning blood. He could detect its curdle in the parasites who said, Come, come little boy, and invited him into the corner; the way it congealed in the veins of fraidycats who smiled for no reason; the way it turned to water in the bodies of those who played the same heartache on the jukebox, over and over again; the way it dried out like a stone in lowlifes just aching to throw down.

Every night Lobo went back to the place where he boxed down, to stare at the cardboard and feel his words grow.

He started writing songs about stuff that happened to others. He knew nothing of love but he'd heard stories, so he'd mention it amid wisdom and proverbs, give it a beat, and sell it. But it was all imitation, a mirror held up to lives overheard. And tho he suspected there was more he could do with his songs, he didn't know how to go deeper. It had all been said before. Why bother. All he could do was wait, carry on and wait. For what? A miracle.

It was exactly as he'd always envisioned palaces to be. Supported by columns, paintings and statues in every room, animal skins draped over sofas, gold doorknockers, a ceiling too high to touch. And more than that, it was people. So many people, striding down corridors. This way and that, attending to affairs or looking to shine. People from far and wide, from every corner of the earth, people from beyond the desert. Word of God there were even some who had seen the sea. And women who walked like leopards, and giant warriors, their faces decorated with scars; there were Indians and blacks; he actually saw a dwarf. Lobo sidled up to circles, he pricked up his ears, thirsting to learn. He heard tell of mountains, of jungles, of gulfs, of summits, in singsong accents entirely new to him: yesses like shesses, words with no esses, some whose tone soared up so high and sank so low it seemed each sentence was a journey: it was clear they were from nowhere near here.

He'd been out this way long ago, when still with his parents. But back then it was a dump, a hellhole of waste and infection. No way to know it would become a beacon. The royalty of a king determined these things: the man had settled among simple folk and turned the filth to splendor. Approached from afar, the Palace exploded from the edge of the desert in a vast pageantry of gardens, gates and walls. A gleaming city on the fringes of a city in squalor, a city that seemed to reproduce its misfortune on street after street. Here, the people who came and went thrust their shoulders back with the air of those who know that theirs is a prosperous dominion.

The Artist had to find a way to stay.

He'd learned there was to be a party that night, set off for the Palace, and played his only card.

"I come to sing for the chief."

The guards glanced at him like a stray dog. Didn't even open their mouths. But the Artist recognized one from the cantina encounter and could tell that the man recognized him, too.

"You saw he liked my songs. Let me sing for him and it'll be good for you, watch."

The guard wrinkled his brow a few seconds, as if imagining his fortune. Then he approached the Artist, shoved him to the wall and frisked. Satisfied that he was harmless, the guard said:

"He better like you." Then dragged him in, and when the Artist was on his way, he warned, "Round here, you blow it, you're fucked."

Finding no good space for himself at the party he thought it better to wander among the guests. Until the music started and a sea of sombreros rose up, looking for action on the dance floor. Couples configured and the Artist found himself ricocheted from hips and elbows. Some fiesta, he thought. He'd scoot to one side and a couple would come at him in three quick steps, scoot to the other and the next one tripped him on a turn. Finally he managed to corner himself and take it in without getting in the way: so elegant, the sombreros; so suave, the violence with which those thighs pressed together; and so much gold, dripping off the guests.

Awestruck, the question took him by surprise.

"Like what you see, amigo?"

The Artist turned and saw a blondish man, weathered and elegant, who sat in his chair giving him a What Do You Think? face. He nodded. The man pointed to an empty seat beside him and outstretched his hand.

He said his name and then stressed:

"Jeweler. All the gold you see, I made. You?"

"I make songs," the Artist replied. And no sooner was this out of his mouth than he sensed that he, too, could begin repeating, after his name: Artist, I make songs.

"Have a drink, amigo; plenty here to get you going."

Yes, indeed, it was a banquet. On every table was whiskey, rum, brandy, tequila, beer, and plenty of sotol; no one could complain about the hospitality. Girls in black miniskirts topped glasses the moment they were raised, or if you wanted you could go over to a table and pour as much as you liked. The promise of carne asada and roast kid hung in the air as well. A waitress put a beer in his hand, but he didn't so much as touch it.

"Now don't go thinking they paint it red here all the time," said the Jeweler. "The King prefers kicking it with the people, in old saloons, but today's a special day."

He glanced side to side before leaning conspiratorially toward the Artist, tho everybody knew:

"Two kingpins coming in to make a deal and he's got to treat them right, go all out."

The Jeweler leaned back in his chair, smug, and the Artist once more nodded and looked around. He felt no envy for the gold-worked belt buckles and snakeskin boots the guests had on, tho they were dazzling; but the outfits the musicians on stage wore, those were something else: black and white spur-print shirts with leather fringe. There by the band, close enough to make requests, he spotted the King, majesty chiseled into his stone cheekbones. He was laughing raucously with the two Lords flanking him, both of whom might have given the impression of power, but no, not the force or commanding air of the King. There was one more man at their table, one who'd also been there at the cantina the other day. Less elegant than the Lords, or more round-the-way: no sombrero, no buckle.

"That's the Top Dog," said the Jeweler, seeing where he was looking. "The King's right-hand man. Punk's got balls, fearless as they come, but he's cocky as shit."

Better be, if he's the Heir, the Artist thought.

"But don't say I said so, amigo," the Jeweler went on, "no gossip allowed. Way it works here is, you make nice with the pack, you'll do fine. Like you and me right now, we just made friends, right?"

Something in the Jeweler's tone put the Artist on edge, and now he did not nod. The Jeweler seemed to sense this and changed the subject. Told him he made jewelry only to order, whatever his clients wanted, and that's what you should do, too, Artist, make everyone look good. The Artist was about to respond when the guard who'd let him in approached.

"It's time," he said. "Hustle up, and ask the boys to accompany you."

The Artist stood nervously and walked to the stage. On the way he sensed the shape and the scent of a different sort of woman but refused to turn his head and look, tho the heat lingered. He stood among the musicians, said Just follow my lead, and launched in. People already knew the story, but no one had ever sung it. He'd asked endless questions to find out what went down, to compose this song and present it to the King. It told of his mettle and his heart, put to the test in a hail of bullets, and had a happy ending not only for the King but also for the down-and-outs he kept under his wing. Beneath that enormous vaulted ceiling his voice projected, taking on depths it never had in the cantinas. He sung his song with the faith of a hymn, the certainty of a sermon, and above all he made sure it was catchy, so people would learn it with their feet and their hips, and so they, too, would sing it later.

When he was done, the crowd showered him with whistles and applause, the elegant musicians clapped him on the back and the Lords accompanying the King headbobbed in contentment and pooched their lips in – the Artist hoped – envy. He climbed down to pay his respects. The King looked him in the eye and the Artist bowed his head.

"I knew you had talent as soon as I saw you," said the King, who, it was known, never forgot a face. "All your songs that good, Artist?"

"I do my best, sir," the Artist stammered.

"Well, don't hold back, then: write; stick with the good guys and it'll all go your way." He nodded to another man standing nearby and said, "Take care of him."

The Artist bowed again and followed the man, fit to burst into tears and blinded by bright lights and his future. Then he took a deep breath, said to himself, It's really happening, and came back down to earth. That was when he remembered the silhouette that had caught his attention. He looked around. And at the same time, the man spoke.

"I'm the Manager. Take care of accounts. You never ask Señor for money, you ask me. Tomorrow I'll take you to a man who does the recording. You give him everything you write," the Manager stopped, seeing the Artist's eyes wander. "And don't stick your snout where it doesn't belong; don't even look at a woman who doesn't belong to you."

"Who does that one belong to?" The Artist pointed to a trussed-up girl to cover his tracks.

"That one," said the Manager like he was distracted, like his mind was on something else, "belongs to who-ever needs her."

He turned back to the Artist, measuring him up, then called the girl over and said, "The Artist here has made Señor very happy; treat him well."

And falling prey to an absurd panic, fearful of what he sensed was about to happen, but more fearful of succumbing to that other aroma, the Artist accepted the Girl's delicate hand and allowed himself to be led from the hall.

What was all that about having been here before, in another life? About God having a chosen path for each of us, since the start of time? For a while, the idea kept the Artist up nights, until he beheld an image in the Palace that freed him: an exquisite apparatus, a turntable with diamond stylus that played thirtythrees and belonged to the Jeweler, who one weekend forgot to turn it off, and, when he noticed two days later, found it no longer worked.

That's it, thought the Artist. That's all we are. Contraptions that get forgotten, serve no purpose. Maybe God put the needle on the record and then went off to nurse a hangover. The Artist already had clear that there was no one high in the sky or down underground looking out for him, that it was each to their own, but now, at the Court, he was starting to see that you could have a little fun before the diamond turned to dust. Not just wait around.

The gift the King had given him days earlier was the sign: his wait was over.

The Girl's blood was a delicate brook trickling over pebbles, but her body inclined to an uncommon skill that took the Artist's breath away for two days straight. You're learning, she'd say, and after each swoon he'd want to drop dead or get married, and would weep. The girl portended so much world, even in the farflung way she spoke, and she'd laugh: I just gave you a nudge and out came a stud, songman. She, too, had been saved by the King; rescued from a hovel by the bridge and brought to the Palace. Now the Girl named her enthusiasm with words newly learned:

"It's amped here, singer, it's trick as shit; man, it's all sauce; it's wicked, slick, I mean this place is *tight*; people here come from everywhere and everybody's down."

How she thirsted for happiness, but the Artist could see in her eyes that she also yearned for other affections, for things not found in the Palace.

For the first few days almost all the Artist did was eat. From the start, he would show up in the dining room when the guards were being fed and share their rations. But all that did was awaken a hunger that had long since skulked within. The Girl told him to do as she had, when she first arrived with a stomach empty for years: turn up as soon as the King, who also ate there – occasionally even with the others – was done, and finish anything he'd left untouched. There were always several dishes, and the chef allowed them to be eaten provided nothing was taken out of the hall.

Spending so much time there, the Artist began to hear the stories people told as they lingered over the table after mealtime, and he used them to weave the fabric of his songs.

"Fools take me for a chump, I lose my shit," one said. "The other week a mule tried to short me, so I took a pair of pliers and tore off his thumbs. No need to kill him, but at least now he'll have a hard time counting his cash. Shitbag deserved it for playing dirty, right?"

"Deep down, I'm a sentimental guy," said another. "So to keep track of the dogs I smoke, I pull a tooth from each one and stick it in my dashboard; wonder how many smiles I'll end up with in my truck."

They loved each other like brothers, they scratched each other's bellies, they gave each other nicknames. One was a guard who'd been caught poking a calf so they called him the Saint, since animals loved him.

"Damn, Saint, you're sick," they taunted, "I just realized this barbecue tastes like you."

Some poor fatty who'd had his arms ripped off as payback now worked there as a messenger; he wore a backpack and roamed the Palace making deliveries. They called him Danger Boy and when the guards saw him coming they'd shout, "Danger! Danger!" And Danger Boy would laugh.

The Artist realized that people saw him only when he sang or they wanted someone to hear how tough they were; and that was good, because it meant he could see how things worked in the Court. Like a cat in a new house, he gradually began to venture out beyond the dining hall and the Girl's room. He got lost constantly. The Palace was a simple grid with a courtyard at the center but there were so many unpredictable corridors that sometimes when he thought he was headed one way, he'd end up at the other end of the building. To keep from being overwhelmed by the Palace's grandiosity, the Artist began carrying one of the Girl's tiny mirrors, observing details over his shoulder: carved furniture, metal doors, candelabras. That was also how he was able to observe, unnoticed, visitors from the cities, suits with briefcases, officers of the law who'd come for their kickback, the business never ended. It was like being invisible.

He discovered that in addition to the King, his guards, the girls and the servants, several courtiers lived there as well. The one he always bumped into was the Manager, ever busy ensuring things ran smoothly. He took him to meet a band that was to record his lyrics so he could make sure the songs came out the way he'd heard them in his head; he even recorded a song himself.

"Then the Journalist will promote your music with his contacts on the radio," the Manager said.

The Artist went back to his digs only once, to keep the dogs from taking over his box; but since no one seemed to notice him at the Palace, or else they'd grown used to him, he brought his few belongings – a notebook with his songs, a dressy vest – and settled in.

To no courtier did he deny his talents. He wrote a corrido for the house Gringo, a master at devising routes for product. The Gringo had cozied up to a gang of young buzz-seekers who crossed over every Friday to kick it this side of the wall. You got a caretaker in me, you sure do; they trusted. The wildest one was a freckled kid, son of a Consul who the Gringo would send back home with fatherly affection and car seats stuffed with weed. Nice little setup, till freckles got lost in a fleapit shooting gallery. Top-notch corrido. He wrote one for the Doctor, the Court's Número Uno stitch-it man, who the King sent to treat a triggerman that got shotgunned in the stomach. The punk was double-crossing, but didn't know they knew. The Doctor eased his pain but also slipped in a gift for the shits he worked for. So when the two-timer went to see his handlers, the poison in his belly blew up on cue and brought them all down, no glory. He wrote one for Pocho, the guy with gringo airs who used to say, as if it were his name: I didn't cross the border; the border crossed me. Pocho had been a cop on the other side but one day he found himself in a jam, and justice shone its light on him: three of his men had surrounded the King, who was prepared to die with honor rather than go down, but a snitch came up to Pocho and said, Who says you got to be on their side? So he emptied his clip into the uniformed thugs, and has been with the good guys ever since.

To no courtier did he deny his talents, but the Artist recounted the feats of each man without forgetting who made it all possible. Sure, you're down, because the King allows it. Sure, you're brave, because the King inspires you. The only time he didn't mention the King's name was when he wrote little love songs that some courtier requested in hushed tones. After, they'd slap him on the back or hook his neck and say, Whatever you want, Artist. Of course he also couldn't use the King's name when he wrote words for little jobs requiring letters. Things like We're sending our cop, so don't sweat the authorities – and he knew to spell authorities au; or Write your personal details here, on a bogus passport. The Artist knew how to make himself useful. And knew how to gain respect: if he said Not just now, I'm working on a corrido, the courtiers listened.

Only two men in the Court didn't ask for corridos. And damn if they didn't deserve them. He saw them together on a Palace balcony tossing back a couple of whiskeys. When he told the Heir he had a story almost ready for him, the man said:

"Later." Clenched his jaw as if holding back the words that followed and simply repeated, "Later."

He was spine-chilling, the Heir, with his impeccable solid-colored shirts, never a single stain, tho his eyes foretold explosion. The man contained himself as if always on his best behavior.

And the other one who declined, the Journalist, the man who maintained the King's good name, said:

"Better not, because if you paint my picture then I'm no use. Imagine: if people on the outside find out I'm on the inside, who's going to believe I don't know what's what?"

The Artist understood. He had to let the man do his job. In order to keep fools entertained with clean lies, the Journalist had to make them seem true. But the real news was the Artist's job, the stuff of corridos, and there were so many yet to sing that he could forget whatever didn't serve the King.

"No offense," the Journalist said, "I don't mean to insult you. And since you like to write so much, I'm going to bring you some books, if I may."

The Artist could feel his guts seize up in excitement, but he was good at concealing things so you couldn't tell.

"You'll love them, just wait," said that Journalist. "When a person likes words, they're like booze for your ears."

Just then all three turned their heads, because down the hall came the King, at a furious pace, looking haggard. He was followed by a woman with long gray hair and a long dress; badass, with a blistering air. The King stopped for a second, turned to look as tho surprised to see them there, then continued on his way and entered the room at the end of the hall. It's time, the woman said, and then followed him. They slammed the door.

The Artist hadn't seen him since the day of the dance. He hadn't missed the King's presence because the King was always present: in the devotion with which he was mentioned; in his orders, which were all carried out; in the luster of the place.

"There they go," said the Journalist, pulling on his drink. "This about the Traitor or is it the same old thing?"

The Heir gripped his glass and nodded but seemed to be responding to nothing.

"That witch," he finally mumbled. And then, when it seemed he wasn't going to add anything else: "But things are changing."

The Artist, who knew to keep his mouth shut, gazed out at the desert and didn't move until he knew that the others had gone back into the Palace. Then with feline patience, he stared at the door the King and the Witch had disappeared behind. Not a sound. He approached, trying to see shadows in the light streaming under the door, pressed his ear. Nothing. He *knew* he shouldn't go in, but his urge beat out his fear and, heart pounding, he went to open the door, stopping his hand just before it touched the handle and jerking it back as tho he'd been burned.

He went to find the Girl. On the way to her room he caught whiff of the same scent as the other night, and on turning a corner the aroma came to life for a few seconds: first it hit him like a gust of insolence, eyes that devoured him then spat him out; then it was harmony, long hair pulled back and a spine that curved in the start of a curl; and then a sudden frost that numbed his gut. He kept walking, instinctively, without thinking, floating, and when he got to the Girl asked mechanically about the intrigue, though he'd already forgotten it. She said:

"They say there's some hotshit who didn't like the new deal, I don't know; I heard he's selling in the plaza without the King's permission. Can you believe that? Idiotic, disturbing the peace like that . . . What's wrong?"

The Artist took a deep breath and this time asked the question that was really on his mind:

"Who is she?"

No clarification required. The Girl sat in fuming silence for a few seconds and then said:

"Some commoner. A tramp."

They are. There. So many letters together. His. Put there for no reason but to penetrate his brain. They are. There. Milling the sheets between rolls of insomnia, they signal, scratching at the wasted white of the paper, at his eyes. And what was each sheet if not a working tool, like a saw for someone who builds tables, a gat for someone who takes lives? Ah, but never this bluff of sand, the spirit and ambition to uncover. So many letters there. They are. There they are. They are a glimmer. How they jostle together and overflow, soaking each other and enveloping his eyes in an uproar of reasons. No matter if they're perfect, or unruly, they incriminate, fearing disarray: words. So many words. His. An uproar of signs bound together. They are a constant light. There. They are. (Books were something he already knew about, but they had spurned him, like an unwelcoming country. And now he'd let himself be led by the hand to the council of secrets. A constant light.) Each with its own radiance, each speaking the true name in its own way.

Even the most false, even the most fickle. Aha. No. Not just there to penetrate his brain. There. They are a constant light. The way to other boxes, far away. The road to ears hidden right here. (Like the bugs that bite him.) No. Not just there to amuse his eyes or entertain his ear. They are a constant light. They are the lighthouse flare cast over stones at his command, they are a lantern that searches, then stops, and caresses the earth, and they show him the way to make the most of the service that is his to render.

It was like an omen: the day they skewered Pocho's head the pain that had wracked the Artist's own since he was a kid came back full force. Hit him like a two-by-four, knocked him out. Even the cricket chirps were deafening and no witches' brew could ease the pain. At the Girl's alarm the Doctor came, inspected the Artist's pupils in search of diagnosis. Leave me, Doc, leave me, it'll pass, said the Artist; and the Doctor asked When did it start and how often and brought on by what, and prescribed pills to soothe him and said:

"You need tests, I'll talk to the Manager so he can fix it up with the hospital, meanwhile, take the medicine."

Screw the medicine, no way was the Artist going to take it, not him. He wouldn't even drink tepid water. He knew: Deal with it, this is just the way it is. Let others find elixirs for their sorrows or pains, he was no judge; but he chose to govern his insides on his own. He'd already had his go at tinctures: smack from some well-off drunks, the kind who are fast friends after a bottle and three songs. The Artist had lost all sense of distance, and music – his music – sounded like moaning. It scared him so bad not to know his own body that he resolved: no venom, no matter what. He handpatted at the Doctor to say Sure, sure, so that the man would leave him alone, and fell asleep.

Hours later he awoke with the terrifying clarity that told him, from the second he heard the first screams: something awful was going down.

He followed the frantic mob to the Palace gates. And before he saw Pocho's body, the Artist sensed the crowd's fear. Very few voices broke the courtiers' petrified silence, swearing as they stood beside the body. His eyes were open and his arms crossed as though he were cold. A curved dagger went in one ear and out the other, with almost no blood. There was no bag or blanket, as usual, and they hadn't tied his hands, nor could you see any singemarks from the wires used to make men talk. Behind the throng came the King with his retinue. The Heir shouted, loud, and the sea of rubberneckers parted. The King observed Pocho. He stood there awhile, hands on his waist, with the expression of a man who wished he hadn't already seen it all. Then he said:

"Take him in." And strode back to the Palace.

The Heir stayed back to ask: Who was on guard, What was the truck like, How many were there, And you, what did you do. Not a soul had seen a thing. He ordered two of the guards to be taken in to make sure they didn't know more than they said and then left. Cold. Too calm for all that rage, thought the Artist. But I bet he knows what he's doing. He, too, followed the entourage to the Palace chapel, where the Doctor was extracting the dagger from Pocho and saying: Never seen anything like it. Then the Father arrived. The Artist hadn't met him yet, tho he knew of the services he lent the Court in exchange for the King's money, funding churches to get the poor hooked on heaven. Those in hats took them off and made the sign of the cross. The Father blessed Pocho quietly and then said, louder:

"What path is this we're on?"

The courtiers said Amen tho it was out of place, and then the King entered. Without waiting for the order almost everyone filed out, and just the Witch, the Father, the Heir and the Gringo remained in the room. The Artist stood back in the shadows and kept quiet.

"This was those bastards from the south," said the Gringo. The Traitor could never have pulled this off alone; they have to be backing him."

"If they want war, give it to them," said the Witch, who was the only one not looking at the corpse but at the King's eyes, her gaze a tense rope.

The King bent over and brushed his fingers through Pocho's hair, said something to him without speaking, just moving his lips. Suddenly he turned to the Heir. How do you read this?

"We can take down whoever we need to," he said, "but what if that's what they're looking for? Whose interests are served by a war? Not ours, I tell you that."

"Coward!" spat the Witch. "They bring a body to your door and you don't retaliate? Those traitors challenge your Lord and you do nothing?"

The Heir cut her off. "That's not the way we kill," pointing to Pocho's wound, "which means that's not the way they kill. You ask me, this is about something else."

"Listen," the King stepped in, addressing the Gringo, "you're going to find out what else Pocho was into on the other side. We've got to make sure we get it right, don't want to find out this was payback for some shit from back in the day. Meanwhile, find me the Traitor, he's in for it anyway, but don't bring him down till I say so."

"If we wait . . . " the Witch protested, but the King interrupted her.

"I said we wait. You don't know war."

Like saying shut up. The King took the Father by one shoulder and said:

"Bury him for me, the Manager will give you what you need for the box."

"And what I still need for my ranchito . . . " the Father slipped in. The King nodded, turned and left the chapel.

The others followed, with the exception of the Father. The Artist emerged from the shadows and stood beside him.

"Probably deserved it," said the Father to Pocho's remains.

The words made the Artist flinch, like a slap. He left the chapel without a word, hoping that it would be taken as an affront but knowing that it wouldn't, since he was invisible; but the Father's lack of judgment offended him. If he knew one thing it was that in the course of life, sooner or later, you cause pain, and it was better to decide up front who you cause it to, like the King. Who was brave enough to accept it? Who bore the cross for the rest? He was their mantle, the wound that took the pain that others may not hurt. They couldn't fool the Artist: he had grown up suffering at the hands of badge and uniform, had endured the humiliation of the well-to-do – until the King came along. So what if the man moved poison when they asked for it on the other side? Let them have it. Let them take it. What had they ever done for the good guys?

"Probably deserved it," the Artist hissed in rage, and then thought: if there's one thing we deserve, it's a heaven that's real.

The boss was coming back, the one they'd done a deal with, and to keep spirits up, the King arranged amusements. No only were the guests supplied with hooch, smack and women, but they set up a casino and organized a shooting contest.

The whole Court moved to the grounds. They brought cages with dozens and dozens of doves, black ones that wouldn't get lost in the desert glare. The King, the Heir and the other boss and his top dog positioned themselves, shotguns aimed up at the sky. Each marksman had a guard in charge of fetching the pieces he shot and putting them in a sack behind him. The cages were opened and suddenly there came a great skyward flutter and a hail of bullets. The crowd clapped each time the shooters hit a bird and it fell, leaving a dark trail.

The boss was a good shot, even allowed himself the luxury of taunting his birdboy, firing at his feet while shouting:

"Ándele, ándele, ándele, bastard, time to earn your keep."

The spectators whooped at his antics, while the boss – laughing his head off, hardly taking aim and not stopping to see if he'd hit – fired his gun nonstop, up and down, sky and ground. The fetchers to'd and fro'd with the pieces, sometimes squabbling, ripping a bird. Even then it was clear that the King, tho he took careful aim and almost always hit his mark, was not fast enough, and he was losing.

A sequence of images flew through the Artist's brain in quick succession: the King defeated, the scorn and petulance of the no-account winner, the faces of the Courtiers – dejected, when yet again it rained on their parade. More than a reflex, his reaction was an instantaneous understanding of how he could be of service. He scooted out in front of the spectators and, while everyone was gazing at the hullabaloo up above, edged over to the King's sack while his fetcher was out in the field. The Artist crouched and pulled a bird from the bag and then stood there, waiting, until the King turned and, utterly astonished, saw what he was doing. Then the Artist sidestepped repeatedly, his back still to the crowd, until he was at the capo's sack. Now he waited for the capo to see him and then swiftly, wearing a guilty face, chucked that same bird into his sack. There was one more cage to go, but the boss was no longer laughing; instead he'd turned to stare at each sack between shots. When there were no more doves in the sky, the kingpin approached the King.

"What the – ?" he asked, face uncomprehending.

The King lifted his chin a bit: what are you on about? The boss then demanded:

"Show me your hands."

The Artist held them out, bloody, and the King wiped off his innocent expression, burst out laughing as though he'd just gotten the joke, and clapped the capo on the back.

"Don't be angry, friend, it's just that my boy here told me you'd been given a faulty shotgun by mistake." The King opened his arms wide and added, "And that's not how we roll here. At my house the guest always wins."

The capo stood in suspense, as if waiting for a conclusion to draw itself. Then his laughter grew louder and louder, and he embraced the King.

"Sly fox! They told me you were a gentleman." And he turned to the public and pointed to the King: "This is your winner! This is your winner right here!"

The public applauded without having heard what the bosses had said, happy because they seemed happy. The King beamed in his blue shirt with bright reds and yellows. He invited the boss to a game of poker and the crowd trailed after to the casino. But halfway there he stopped and turned, hands on hips, gazing intently at the Artist, his face one of surprise and satisfaction.

"So you're a crafty bastard," he whispered, and turned back to the Palace.

"So, does a girl have to carry a gun for you to write her a song?" said she, the Commoner.

Staring at him. She was staring right at him, and the Artist didn't know how to handle the astonishment he felt with her almond eyes trained his way. He stood frozen until she arched her eyebrows like this – Well . . . ? – as though aiming a cannon at his chest, and then he replied.

"It's not about the guns, it's the stories. What's yours?"

"I don't tell the truth to anyone in this place," she said, and started walking back down the hall that the Artist had ended up on. The Artist followed a little ways, finding and discarding the precise words he needed to prolong their conversation. They went out to the grounds, strolled by a fountain in whose center stood a god spitting water through its mouth, carried on to a maze of shrubs that spelled out the King's name, and on reaching a swimming pool tiled in mosaic made to look like leaves and grass, the Artist got it right.

"So don't tell the truth, tell me lies."

The Commoner turned and stared for a second, astonished. She leaned over the water as if searching for someone to take it out on. Then she gazed out at the perimeter, the electrified fence, the desert; and after awhile she said:

"What's the point? You might end up believing me."

They walked to where the King's collection was. There were snakes, tigers, crocodiles, an ostrich and, in a bigger cage, almost its own garden, a peacock.

"His favorite," said the Commoner, swooping out an open hand, ironic. The animal flapped its wings and the Artist saw that it had a small bandage around its foot. He was about to ask how the animal got wounded there and who took the time to treat it, but the Commoner said:

"I need to go see my mother." Seeing the question in his eyes she added, "The one who's always with him."

The Artist shivered a bit at the hatred with which she'd referred to the witch, and more at the confirmation that they were blood. He opted not to follow her when she returned to the Palace as if she'd been out alone. Still, tho she'd turned her back to him, she had left a trail of pebbles with which to find her: rage and secrets; she'd looked at him.

The days that followed would have been the happiest in the Artist's life since his encounter with the King were it not for the fact that they were also the most unsettled. Suddenly his lyric urge abandoned him and his ear served only to listen for the Commoner's footsteps, his eyes only to surveil corners, his hands only to tremble at her absence. But he pretended. He aped the self that kept its cool.

When he came across the Commoner he stuck to her side and they spoke on the go: she wore loose men's pants and uncinched shirts, hiding her body, but when she moved the cloth and her skin met and the Artist could see it. They almost never sat, and when they did the Commoner would sink into her chair as if impressing her shape.

That was the way they roamed the Palace. Treacherously, the Artist slowly learned her curves as they ran through topics and rooms. In the ballroom he grazed her forearm and told her of his parents on the other side of the line; in the game room he brushed her back with an elbow as she spoke of when she'd had friends, as a girl; in the armory he stroked her hair and told her stories of cantinas – but the topic made her stop listening, for some reason she switched off and slowly began to close her eyes, curling up like a kitten, and the Artist felt the urge to accompany her silence, for in it he understood her a little better; when they spoke of the Witch his thigh glanced her thigh as they rambled around the boardroom with built-in cantina, the study with built-in cantina, the balcony with built-in cantina, the dining room with built-in cantina, and the cantina proper, so magnificent.

"She frees him of a demon," said the Commoner. And she told him how, long ago, when he was not yet who he would become, the King had asked her mother for help and the two of them had left her father, a good man who was therefore a useless man, and now a lonely man.

From that moment on, the soundtrack of his desire took on a strident tone, because he realized he had no permission to touch the Commoner: the King had not consented, and without his say-so things could never move forward. He had gotten close to the Commoner because he took the Girl at her word when she'd said that that was what she was: one of many. And now what was he doing? Not only longing to touch her but to be with her, to share her solitude. He stood at a distance when they strolled but could not calm his trembling. She knew it when he stared at her perfect little nose, aching to trace a finger across her eyebrows.

"If there's a fly on my face, get it off," the Commoner said, and the Artist hid his hands like a thief. She laughed tenderly, perhaps, and then led him to a room lined with empty shelves.

"The library," she stated with absolutely no emphasis, as tho she hadn't said anything at all. Yes, there were a few sheets of paper, a bible, maps, newspapers with stories of dead men, a magazine with a color photo of the members of the Court at a wedding. Mentally, the Artist unfolded a scrap of paper on which he scribbled the idea for a song about the King and his men planning war.

Soon the Artist began sweating distress, because he could feel the Commoner's body getting closer: as they gamboled by the Girl's room, which at the time was still his, too, she sunk her nails lightly into his waist; passing the guards' barracks she pressed her face to his at the slightest pretext; in the trucks' loading bay he endured the tips of her breasts pointing against his back. That very afternoon he decided to take off the brakes, to find her and come undone in confessions. He caught sight of her on the same balcony where he'd heard the Heir and the Journalist scheming, set off so she couldn't get away, and a few meters before he reached the corner where there was nothing but the balcony and the locked room, felt someone jerk his shoulder.

"I was looking for you," the Journalist said. "There's a problem with your songs."

The Artist turned to fling off the hand that restrained him, looked at the spot where he should have found the Commoner, and a second before he could confirm it, knew that he wouldn't find her, knew that there, people disappeared.

They didn't want his songs. Jockeys at the station said his words were coarse, his good guys were bad. Or they said yes, but no: they liked the lyrics but had orders to shut his groove down. It wasn't the Artist's unbuttery voice, he'd only recorded one little tune; other singers, finer voices, were tasked with giving his songs a smoother sound. One of the DJs said to the Journalist, hey, between you and me, the Supreme G is turning the screws tight these days: a show for the gringos, temporary hush-hush till the advertisers cool down. Couldn't he ask the Artist to clean it up a little, write sweeter songs, less crude?

"Don't look at me," said the Journalist, "I'm just letting you know, and now I'm taking you to Señor so we can figure out what to do about this . . . He'll be free in a minute."

So they didn't want him, thought the Artist, so he was chump change for the big-money men, so he made their ears itch. He'd been insulted a hundred times before, only this time he wasn't humiliated: he swaggered, felt superior. He clenched his jaw and suddenly could see it all clearly. It was the rejection of others that defined him. Shit, so what if his singing pained them, in the end what the Artist enjoyed was gazing into the eyes of his audience, bringing their bones to life on the dance floor, singing to the people, real people.

His footsteps and those of the Journalist rang out on the marble: an energetic echo. The Artist spouted off under his breath and as the marble sped by underfoot he got madder and madder, and surer of himself, as if the answer lay waiting at the end of the hall. In the Gallery.

"Here we are," said the Journalist.

People lined up, coming in through a big door, in shawls and tattered trousers, carrying kids, their faces blank but shining slightly with faith. The Gallery was a controlled chaos, alarmed yet deferential, and smelled of dirt and salt, and a kind of curdled heat.

"Where were you?" demanded the Jeweler the second he saw him walk in. "Don't you know what today is?"

The Artist didn't know, and felt ashamed since he saw that somehow it was his duty to know, for as soon as he entered and sensed the atmosphere, he got goosebumps and suspected that he was not alone in his anger, that his anger was incarnate.

"Every month there's an audience," the Jeweler explained, "and you have to be present for whatever might arise. Some are only looking for meds, or a job, or payback, but for others, he changes their lives with some little thing: Señor as their baby's godfather, or helping out with a quinceañera. He grants things to them all. And what was he supposed to do if someone asked for a corrido?"

The Artist nodded, suddenly both guilty and excited at the scene. The crowd at the back was a blur, an indistinct mass of gray, but he could clearly see those almost at the front of the line, who stood straight, tugged their hair to the side, kept quiet, did up a button. And at the head, surrounded by the Court, the King looked them each in the eye, listened to the favor requested, motioned to the Manager and the Manager made a note. Some he stroked their hair or counseled in a grave tone of voice. Then they wanted to kiss his hand or embrace his knees, and the King allowed them to adore him for a moment before casting them off with gentle force.

The Jeweler, too, was dazzled by the audience; he, so fine, seemed to flourish at the passion expressed by the simple; outside he likely would have looked straight through them, but here he didn't miss a trick when it came to seeing that Señor worked miracles, and they were transformed.

"That's why we're here," said the Jeweler, "to give him power. By ourselves, what good is any one of us?

None at all. But in here, with him, with his blood, we're strong . . . And let no one think they can take anything from Señor!"

The Jeweler was almost shouting by the end, and the people cowered for a second, until the Journalist slapped him on the back.

"Easy, tiger, easy now."

The Artist tried to distract the Jeweler by asking, "You ever make special pieces for the people?"

"All my pieces are special," he replied, "and all the special pieces you see here were made by me."

For a second the Artist thought the Journalist and the Jeweler exchanged a look of surprise, or that the Journalist was about to fly off the handle, but it was only for an instant, because then the Audience ended.

The King rose and strode toward the hall, the people's pleading looks trickling down to his feet; behind him, the Manager consoled those still in line: Next month, next month.

"Come on," said the Journalist.

They rushed to the back of the royal entourage and the Journalist approached the King.

"Señor, it seems we have a problem with the Artist . . . "

The King stopped, arched an eyebrow.

"Well, not with the Artist, what problem would we have with him," the Journalist grinned, "it's the DJs who have the problem. They won't play his songs."

"Oh? And why's that?" said the King, as if to say, What's new.

"Same old story: they mustn't be seen speaking well of you to the people."

The King glanced back toward the Gallery, to where people were heading home, laden with favors.

"As if we need those asses in order for people to speak of me," he said. "Don't you worry about it, the Manager here will arrange things with our friends to move your music on the street . . . After all, isn't that the way we do business?"

The King looked tired, but also full of restrained power. He smiled, and his smile seemed a protective embrace that said to the Artist, Why sugarcoat the ears of those fuckers? We know what we are and we're good with it. Let them be scared, let the decent take offense. Put them to shame. Why else be an artist?

They're dead. All of them, dead. The others. They cough and spit and sweat their deaths, rotted through with self-satisfied deceit. As if they shat diamonds. They grin with bare teeth, like corpses; like corpses, they figure nothing bad can happen to them.

Word.

They have a nightmare, the others: the men here – the good guys – are their nightmare; the smell here, the noise here, the hustle here. But here it's more real, in the flesh, alive and kicking, and them, they're not even close, nothing but bags of bones, pappyjacks with no color. Pale reflections, lifeless cut-outs, held up by pins.

You don't ask dead men for their say-so. Or at least not dead shitbags. You just do what you do. You swagger and you strut, you speak the name out loud, and don't take any notice if it wigs the others out. Or you do: just to feel their fear, right, because their fear is what you feed off and makes clear that the flesh of the good is brave and necessary, that it shakes things up and fills the space.

They should be snatched up by the hair and have their faces rubbed in that vile truth, that ruthless putrid truthful truth, let them be lured in by it. They should be stuck on the spikes of our sun, drowned in the ruction of our nights, have our songs inserted under their fingernails, be lain bare with our skins. They should be tanned and hided. And caned.

It spooks them to hear talk of their bad dream, which takes words and lives. It spooks them for One to be the sum of all their flesh, to have Him be as strong as all of them together. It spooks them to see who He is and what He's like and how He's named. They only dare to admit it when they abandon themselves to their truths, in juice, in dance, in heat, they're fucked, that's all they're good for. They'd rather hear just the pretty part, but the songs we sing don't ask their say-so, a corrido aint a painting that hangs on the wall to look pretty. It's a name and it's a weapon.

If it spooks them, cool.

Either way. In the end they'll find out they're nothing but maggoty flesh.

Softly, moving from one side of the roof to the other, head rising and dipping, the Artist sang his roughneck song about a rich lady who threw a party at her house. It got crashed by two little bigshots hoping to make their name in the business; looking smooth, the bucks slipped in and hooked a couple of stuckup honeys who were rich and well-to-do, which was the name of the song, "Rich and Well-to-Do", tho, the Artist acknowledged, it could also have been called "Luscious and in Love" or "Left in Love", or at least that's what he thought. So the bigshots started working their silverspoon ladies, using them as mules to cart junk here to there, and man was it perfect cause these girls loved to shake it, and they looked – went the song – like movie stars, tho they were really just corrido queens; thing is, it couldn't last forever, no, not a setup that sweet, because of course they really fell for it, the gear, the front, they wanted it all to come true and started sticking up their noses and watching who they went with, and what good were they then, if

54

changing their ways meant leaving cash on the table? So, psh, what are you going to do? The bigshots stuck the girls on a bus, Be there in a flash, they said, y'all just get off round that bend, but no, no sir, next stop was the other end of the world, and they were sorry as they watched the bus pull out, but there wasn't nothing for it – a job's a job.

He'd struggled to smooth out the song's rough edges, especially at the end, when they realize they got to go it alone. But he had it down now, and once he had it he all of a sudden stopped and looked around the roof and took in the burning Kingdom with his eyes: the long strip of sand surrounding it, the acacia trees, the sky that raced and raced in all directions, one side still bright blue and the other flaming rose, and he thought: far as the eye can see, that's how far the King's reach extends, and with it, my words, and considering this quietly he added: Bastards.

The Artist stayed there until darkness began to eat up all the color, feeling so small and so free, and then he went down. He passed the area where the study was, close to the gallery, then the area where the games room was, skirted the wing where King's quarters lay, close to the terrace, and finally the guards' quarters and the girls' rooms. Though there were corridors he had yet to explore, he no longer struggled to find his way to the Girl in the Palace. She was going to love this song! The Girl hadn't wanted him to write about how when she was little she was sold for a clapped-out car, but with hooks like the ones in his corrido, she would surely see he was making amends for her, too.

He watched her folding clothes on the bed and it filled him with tenderness: her slight waist, her slender shoulders, the taut, pale skin that he'd been so excited to touch in the early days and that now made him want to comfort her and make her happy, even if he couldn't. He slid a finger down the pebbles of her spine. She turned and instead of surprise wore an expression that said Oh, you.

"Listen to what I wrote to get even."

He sang his corrido a cappella.

As he sang, the Artist slapped his thighs and made faces he hoped were witty, but when he saw the Girl's wrath he felt ridiculous. In the end, silence and more silence, brief but unyielding.

"You don't know jack, do you?" she said with scorn.

"What is it I should know?"

The Girl turned her back and kept folding. The Artist began to serenade her, circling as tho taking a stroll through the room. He was giving his best shot at getting the Girl to smile but she wouldn't even glance his way and he saw it was best to stop playing cute. So he kissed her shoulder and headed for the door.

"Come on, fool. What do you think?" she asked before the Artist made his exit, adding, "They're badass motherfuckers and you're nothing but a clown."

The Artist turned, perplexed more at the venom in the Girl's voice than her scorn for him or the way she insulted the King.

"I thought you were happy here."

"That's what we tell all our customers," she shot back bitterly. Then wheeled to face him and said, "Have you heard yourself recently? You talk like every other asshole around here. Making jewels." She jerked her chin up, challenging. "Now step off; I don't want to see you near my bed again."

The Doctor stopped prodding his eye sockets and said sullenly:

"If you refuse to let me examine your head with the proper instruments, I can't tell what the problem is . . . Though I have my suspicions."

This last line he added in a tone both harsh and sad. The Artist wouldn't let anyone near him with a knife or anything like one. They spent the next few seconds in silence: a dialogue of suppressed premonitions. Then the Doctor shook it off with a smile.

"What we can do, in the interim, is take care of the obvious problem." He bent over a desk and took out a box which he set down a few feet from the Artist. "Because it is obvious, even if not to you."

A pyramid of letters and numbers decreasing in size, down to tiny at the base. The Doctor said:

"I haven't used this for a long time; nobody here wants to wear specs. Cover one eye."

The Artist covered his left. The Doctor carried on.

"I'm surprised the courtiers don't spend all day running into each other in the corridors. Read me the letters you see."

"En, jay, gee, kay, three, tea, one, why, are, tea, pee."

"Though now that I think about it, there certainly are some run-ins, as I'm sure you've realized, eh? Next line, other eye."

"Aitch, oh, see, queue, doubleyou, en, zee, ex."

"Good. See, sometimes you get the impression that each man's got his own knife and fork now, altho no one should be thinking about a banquet. Next one, back to the left again."

"Jay, a, two, tea, ess, see, eight, a, zee, eff . . . bee?"

"Close: three. I wish things were like back in the day, but, between you and me, seems like everyone's lost it. Next line."

"Dee, e, why, e, one, are, vee, seven."

"El, not one. See, the Traitor's making deals with the crew from the south, but there's no way to know if that's because he's been told to by someone here. They're different down there, they're new at this, do things on the down low. Next."

"Jay, e, eff . . . ess again, three, why, nine, pee, doubleyou, four, dee."

"Hm. Here we go. So on the one hand, top dog is getting nervous, best not even to go near him when he's all het up like that, boy's been trigger-happy since he was a pipsqueak . . . And on the other, That Woman is there, and who knows what her angle is. Next."

"En, e . . . zee?, e, you, jay, el, en again."

"Tsk, tsk. That's enough. Time to dust this thing off."

The Doctor went back to his desk and pulled out a contraption full of glass slides and wires. He removed and replaced lenses and slid it over the Artist, on his nose. Suddenly the letters on the card were clear, but jumpy. They're jiggling, the Artist said. The Doctor switched lenses again. How bout now? Now they're slurred. More lens changing. Now? The Artist made no reply. He was no longer looking at the letters. The shock of so much new minutiae unsettled him: a slight crispness to the walls, gold dust dancing in the sun's rays. And suddenly: the Heir, standing there in the doorway.

"I *what*?" he asked.

The Artist couldn't help but notice his threads. And now, with these eyes, he saw better what they said: his pants linen not denim; soft, crème-colored shirt, not checkered, no stitching. Like the cut of the cloth revealed what the Heir was made of, told of a past different from the rest, more genteel days, troubled blood, a tense way of being there.

"Nothing. Just giving the Artist here a check-up," the Doctor replied.

The Heir smiled broadly, but it was like an accident on his face.

"Course you are. That's your job," he nodded slowly. "*Your* job, right? Yours and no one else's. Not the Witch's, for example."

He took a few steps in until he stood before the Doctor.

"What is that bitch trying to cure the King of?" He placed his hands on the Doctor's shoulder. "Tell me."

The Doctor met the Heir's gaze for a second, no more, and then his eyes quivered, watering.

"I don't know, I'm just a doctor, I don't know about that sort of thing."

"What sort of thing, Doc? Explain yourself, See, apparently I'm just a dumbfuck who imagines all kinds of stupid shit. A minute ago I thought you were talking about me, but I'm glad I was wrong, cause when I don't know what's going on, I get a little fucked off. So I prefer straight talk."

"I swear I don't know," the Doctor seemed to hunch over himself, a slight tremor rattling through him. "I'm not that close."

The Artist saw goosebumps rise on the Heir's neck, and the first thing he thought was that it was the sort of rage felt by a man with no game in the sack.

"Well, as soon as you find out, you let me know, because you and I *are* that close." He removed his hands and headed for the door. Before leaving, he added, "And don't worry: it's all a question of learning your place before it's too late."

Ever since the Girl kicked him out, the Artist had been bunking in the guards' quarters, slipping into the cot of whoever was on rounds. That night he'd been abruptly awakened by a guard just getting off, but sleep had forsaken him so he decided not to move to the newly abandoned bed. He began to wander through the Palace in search of a spot with enough light to reread the books of stories and poems on loan from the Journalist. Carrying them with him was like walking with a compadre who knew all manner of secrets.

He leaned over a balcony looking out over the courtyard, which had lights on all night, and picked out a garden bed. The Artist was about to head down and get comfortable when he heard the shouting.

"Where? Where?" The Witch appeared from one end, a walkie-talkie at one ear. From the other, just beneath him, emerged a guard, dragging the Commoner.

"Picked her up as she was trying to hitch a ride on a semi," said the guard, clearly overconfident. He stood, waiting. Perhaps thought this was when the Witch would thank him, but all she did was point to where he'd come from: Out. The guard left. The two women gazed at one another in silence for several seconds. Then the Commoner said:

"Those dogs can't go telling me whether I can leave."

The Witch executed a powerful arc with one hand, striking the Commoner down with her slap.

"It's not the dogs who are telling you. It's me."

She crouched, yanked her daughter up and ragdolled her shoulders.

"What the fuck are you trying to pull? Can't you see there is no other train? Is this what I waited so long for?"

She let her go with a weary look but then took her daughter's hands and, more sweetly, said:

"Do you know what's out there? Trash. Here, it's all going to be yours, soon as I fix that man. Sit tight a little longer. When the rich blood I give him puts his seed to rights, you've got to be ready, too. Even if his damn peacock doesn't work I'm going to find a way to leave all of this to you."

"When did I ever say I was interested in this dump?" the Commoner asked, head still bowed. Her mother stood. On doing so she saw the Artist watching, but showed no surprise.

"I didn't see you turn your nose up at it either," she said, "so if you ask me, you are interested. And even if you're not, we're in it up to our necks."

She lifted the Commoner up by one arm, and as she pulled her towards their rooms cast a quick glance back at the Artist.

"You are not going to fuck things up," she said. "No way am I going to let it all be ruined by some deadbeat."

He went with her back to the City.

"I know how to get out without being seen," he told her, and tho he knew it was playing with fire, the way her eyes lit up gave him the confidence to continue. She wanted out so bad she didn't even ask why he offered to escort her.

The Artist led her to the end of one of the gardens and they leapt the fence at a spot he'd seen on a walk where it wasn't electrified because a stream ran beneath.

When they got to the City, the Commoner led him by the hand, as tho he were the one needing to be shown around the cantinas by the bridge. With fairground glee she showed him cherished sights in each one: a jukebox old as dirt, a turtle-eyed barkeep, a wooden bar carved with cuss words, a band whose members were all midgets, a bathroom where women stood to pee. And at places she'd never been to, she still walked in as tho to size up the tables, holding the Artist's sleeve in silence.

The Artist saw pass before his eyes the world that by the belt he'd learned to survive, and could not share the Commoner's delight. He did see new things, tho, or perhaps the same things were revealed with new force, as if he'd had a callus skinned off his eye and now the whole of him absorbed details he'd never before perceived, things that had been blurred like a bad photo. He picked up on the wounded pluck of the girls who worked it solo and the apathy of pimped old pros; he understood the cold felt by the old codger on the floor, moaning but unable to ask for anything; and a sign for a lost little girl brought home the horror of being tortured by cowards. He recognized himself in an ashen boy coaxing squalid notes from a trumpet but could tell this kid had it worse than he ever did, because he had a littler one to look after, curled up on his back. The Artist had never had to look after anyone else.

It's as if there is no right to beauty, he thought, and thought that the city ought to be set alight from its foundations, because in each and every place where life sprouted up through the cracks, it was immediately abused. But then he looked at the Commoner, who stood on the sidewalk, gazing at a hooker without being seen, contemplating the girl as tho embracing her with her eyes, as tho consoling her, and the Artist thought that for an instant, a light more pure was cast down on the slum, and he was privileged to be able to see it.

"Haven't seen you round the way of late, sugarpie," said a voice behind him. "Months. Thought maybe you didn't like what I gave you."

The Artist turned and saw a big-belly flab man, who fingered his belt buckle as he spoke. The Commoner seemed at first to be scared and then to be pissed: her whole body recoiled as tho ready to spring, but all she did was take one step over and stand by the Artist. The man, too, took a step – forward, toward them.

"So . . . how bout a deal? You know, each give the other what they want."

Though he was instantly overcome with fury, the Artist had no idea how to defend anyone and put his hands behind his back to tuck his shirt in, just to do something, as tho gearing up to fight. The man backed up and cactus-armed in fear.

"Hey, hey! Easy, amigo, no need to go taking out your piece. You want her, take her, girls like this are a dime a dozen."

The Commoner wrapped her arms around the Artist from behind and pulled him to the door of a building without letting go of his chest. She shouted an obscenity at the man and then she and the Artist took backward steps, as if entrenching themselves against the city, until they made it through the door. Of the hotel. It was a hotel. They stood a few seconds staring at reception unsure of what to do, and then the Commoner approached the desk, requested a key, and signaled to the Artist to follow.

Once inside the room she undressed herself quickly and him furiously, and then mounted him – cold, focused – and the Artist was struck by something that made him feel miserable: he sensed that she was staring past his face, at the pillow, at the wall. That was why he simply placed his hands gently on her hips and waited. And suddenly she stopped, head bowed, still on top of him.

"I'm not going to apologize," she said, and slid off and lay beside him, "it's just that I don't know how to act with men who seem nice."

They lay in silence. A light bulb abuzz with mosquitoes stained the darkness. The Artist resolved to stop thinking, all he wanted was to be there with the Commoner. And suddenly he knew her blood: it was a faltering current, lurching clear of invisible boulders. The Artist pressed on a vein in the Commoner's arm and traced it to her wrist and back. He reached his other hand across her body and listened to the veins in one thigh. He traveled the skin that covered those fragile channels to the rhythm of her heart. He felt her blood begin to rush and felt his hands become useless, because every inch of her skin foretold another current, a bloodstream. The Artist gazed at her face: a deliberate face; there are faces that seem accidental, but not this face whose parts all rhymed, not this skin like hot sand that sculpted round cheekbones, tiny mouth, teeth biting a lip; not this face that now sang to itself. They loved one another like people lingering over every instant, with the certainty that it was the only way to be alive. And such lassitude, so slowly: no desire to reach the end of this line.

Afterward they walked outside as if enlightened, indifferent to the nonstop action on the street. Someone approached hawking bootleg CDs and the Artist saw that among them was one of his, which meant nothing. The King had kept his word, but this didn't move him. He'd learned more important things that day.

From a cantina they saw the Gringo emerge, staggering. He stared in surprise but betrayed no sense of scandal.

"I thought you were on the other side," said the Artist.

"Been and came back, but it was no use, they don't know jack. Pocho didn't go over anymore; once he turned his back on them, he did all his business on this side. Besides: only thing he was in charge of was getting girls for Señor, for all the good that did. But that," he held a clumsy finger to his lips, "is hush-hush, eh? You didn't see a thing . . . and I didn't either. Didn't see you two here. Better that way. Better not to know, with the shit that's about to hit the fan."

An icy dust swept through the city. The Gringo halfturned, stumbling, zigzagged a few feet, and set his course for a cantina door.

What's out there? What lies beyond it all? Another world standing, face to the sun? A wave with edges rippling out after a stone hits the water? (Could life be a stone hitting the water?)

To see and see and see and not to see: there is no shape, only a tangled mess grown weary of itself. Arrogant face, deadbeat world.

What's out there? What lies beyond the walls of things?

Like this, like this, there's nothing.

Turn your back on this smug cut grass and choose your own mirror: raise it to your eyes and see:

A chilling glimmer, a tiny spiral asking for a chance, a secret obscured in its own dark light. The whole world can be seen in this mirror, each detail a reversible code. Pieces and more pieces falling over themselves asking to be touched, ever-changing skin.

"So tell me how you write a corrido," the Journalist said. "You just tell the story, that's all?"

The Artist knew how but had never articulated it, expertise was like underwear, something concealed out of modesty that you were almost unaware of. And yet now he felt confident enough to expound.

"The story tells itself, but you have to coax it," he replied, "you take one or two words and the others revolve around them, that's what holds it up. Cause if you're just saying what happened, why bother with a song? Corridos aren't only true; they're also beautiful and just. That's why they're so right for honoring Señor."

The Journalist nodded, but seemed unconvinced.

They were on the terrace, having coffee. The Artist was enjoying their chat, so unlike the shakedowns soon to come. He was mastering more and more words thanks to the books the Journalist had given him and refused to take back, even when the Artist insisted.

"That's good," the Journalist said, "that's good for us, the ones who polish his shoes and watch his back, but you're something else; not saying you don't mean it, but what you do is art, amigo, no need to use all your words of praise on Señor."

"Why not? I write about what moves me, and if what moves me are the things the Chief does, then why not?"

"Sure, sure, don't get me wrong, Artist, all I mean is that your thing has a life of its own, one that doesn't depend on all this. It's good that our hellraising serves as inspiration, I just hope you never have to choose. Seems to me like you're pure passion, and if one day you have to choose between your passion and your obligation, Artist, then you are truly fucked."

He felt the Journalist was plucking a chord he'd been hoping to keep quiet. So, cautious, he responded in a way that both concurred and offered resistance:

"Ffft, my songs will outlive me in the end."

The door to the room at the far end opened and there appeared the Witch. Her long white dress made the blood on her fingertips jump out. The whole of her tense, as tho her entire body were a loaded gun.

"What are you doing here?" she spat. "Don't you have anyplace else to waste your time? Think you'll learn something here, digging in like nits? Asswipes. Piss off! Damn you, get out of here! There's nothing to see!"

The Journalist motioned vaguely and stood. The Artist got out of his chair, still bent almost double; frightened, because unlike the majority of the Palace bigwigs, the Witch had looked straight at him, and her eyes burned.

They headed for the guards' dining room. In silence at first, and then the Journalist, as tho feeling the need to apologize to a guest, confided:

"Not so long ago we were all tight, like family, but now, well, they say the alliance with that other boss fell through . . . Plus there's this war on the horizon . . . "

"But can't you go with them, try to set things straight?"

"Not me, a subordinate, no. There are those who can address the King, but I'm not the kind to jump my station." Somberly, he added, "Tho some are, Artist, that's for damn sure: there's that fool struck out on his own, or found himself a new boss, I'm starting to see."

In the dining room they ran into the Heir, who stood grabbing pieces of raw meat from a lone platter. He glanced up at the new arrivals from the far end of the long table, eyed them quickly but said nothing. The Heir brought pieces of meat to his mouth greedily, but with the slow self-assurance of a man who knows no one is going to fight him for a mouthful. They sat at the opposite end of the table as if to carry on with their conversation, but now said not a word.

That look he had, the fatherly affection, the innocence with which he said:

"There's no one I trust the way I trust you." And if that weren't enough, added: "There are those who will never be satisfied, plain and simple; you, on the other hand, know your place and are happy with your lot."

That look he had, attention focused solely on his object, certain that no one else deserved it at that instant; the look of complicity. The way he touched the Artist's shoulder and led him through the grounds to show off his peacock: the easy intimacy, here we are, just you and me, discussing important things. And the cadence: such unflustered steps, the soles of his feet placed carefully on the ground the whole way. It all confirmed: the King speaks the truth. Which one? He was needed, the Artist was to slip into a baptism party nearby, where one of the King's enemies would be. The Artist, much as it would trouble him, was to pass himself off as a dissident and find out if anyone was conspiring from within. The Artist couldn't tell a soul, because – eyes sincere, insisting – he alone could be trusted, and he alone, given his talent, could pull it off. The Artist embraced his mission with faith and honor, even if he did have to shuttle to one corner his doubts about the last thing the King said, which lingered on like background buzz.

"Time has come for you to make yourself useful, Artist."

So he returned once more to the grimy streets of yore. He knew how to keep his mission under wraps as he searched for the rival top dog to sneak him into the reception. No one beat the Artist at the art of being unseen. All he had to do was prick up his ears and circle the word on the street like a buzzard above a dying man, until he found his way to the right joint.

He approached the top dog after watching him for three days, clocking his habits and noting he had a thing for call girls, that he tried to entice them with song. The Artist laid systematic siege, awaiting the exact moment when the dog was feeling fly; not only did the Artist know the requested tune but had prepared a little bonus, set to impress: an easy corrido, puffed up and swaggering, exalting the exploits he'd heard about the guy.

"Not bad, ace," said the top dog, trying not to let on that he'd liked the song, "but tell me: you already got someone to flatter, no?"

"Used to, but that place is going from bad to worse, truth is I'm looking to make a move."

"That a fact? Don't try me on, cause I can spot a bigmouth a mile off."

The Artist puckered his lips, pooched them out, and said, "Go ahead, search mine."

The punk laughed and feted the joke with much table-slapping.

"Hooo! If it's true you're just a singer, long as your voice don't dry up, it's all good. I'll take you to my boss, like a present. Can you write him a song?"

The Artist wrote more than one, he wrote corridos of friendship for the enemy capo, so fawning they seemed to say he was the true king. Fortunately, they didn't ask for any that criticized the King, but even singing for the other man made something between the Artist's belly and chest burn, a kind of pain he didn't recognize; to keep it from turning him sour he kept telling himself that to lie for Him was worth it, it was.

He plowed gently through the party, sure of where to stand, who to mark, when to speak. He had it down. This party, too, had its jangling gold, its blondes, its red anteater boots, had a band on a stand and a roast, had plenty of hooch, guards, a priest in its pocket. And the Artist set out to find the tête-à-tête that would let him in on the scheming. There were many: the old man scheming against his wife, three girls scheming against their bridesmaid dresses, two roughnecks against a moneyman, a priest against his urge to down the *sotol*; but none led him out of the dark. It was all just like the Court.

The Artist looked and looked with the specs the Doc had sent him, and what jumped out at him was this: *it was all the same.* He could feel the fiesta dribbling by him at the rate of routine. The only odd one there was him, who was seeing it all from outside. The only *special* one was him. It was so beautiful to see that, like a soft glow among the people, like the feeling that things get better when you walk into the room. And as he sang his corridos for the other king, a lightskinned cat lacking grace but sporting tux, the Artist was so smooth that it should have scared him to see how easy it was to feel at home in the role of a man with no blood debt. And there, at that moment, the buzz that had been troubling him since the King's command disappeared. The King's face appeared to him in all its detail, as if under a magnifying glass, and he saw how flaccid the skin, how precarious his constitution, like that of anyone here in this place. He pretended not to be thunderstruck by the discovery. He decided to leave, but before finding the exit had the wherewithal to pick up on a man talking at the bar, whom he examined carefully for a fraction of a second, enough to take in his fine suit, enough to realize that it was the same dog from the newspaper photos in the library, always beside the other man, equally as elegant.

The music cranked up all at once, right from the getgo, with the first *ay*, and then the voice carried the melody, the bass bumped up and down as if spellbound by the beat, the accordion swooped down low on the verses and sped up at the curves; and all the while the drum, solemn, held its own.

> *Ay*, this is a sad corrido
> That tells the story of my King
> A man everybody envies
> For his proud and noble reign
>
> King, your man got whacked
> They stuck a rod right through his crown
> Smoked another with a gat
> Seems to be the latest thing
>
> Some dogs just want to leg it
> And some conspire against you

Tho it's you who took them in
Gave them cash and loved them true

The boys that care bout you are down
Because they see you looking low
But we're all a family
And I won't let you go

They say you were real sick
Meanwhile your boys began to fight
But I don't think you ever said
You didn't need us in your life

Some dogs just want to run
While some conspire against you
Tho it's you who made them rich
Gave them peace and loved them true

Tho you don't say it, King, I know
You don't want us getting shot
Cause you're not made of stone
And we're the only sons you've got

He's our father and a King
And I swear to you he's good
On his turf you damn well best
Be working for the kingdom

Some kingdom cons just want to run
While some conspire against you
Cause you gave them more than cash
You gave them your ambition too

He scribbled the lyrics furiously almost the moment he
left the reception, leaning against the bar in a cantina.
And before passing his new corrido on to his colleagues,
the Artist felt the kind of sparks that fly when you hurtle
downhill in a truck; and felt as if he'd let something go.

On his way back to the Palace he asked himself what would happen if he simply turned another way, any way that wasn't the one he already knew. Ever since arriving at Court he'd been surprised by people's urge to cross the line, or to go to some other city, even if it was on this side. Not even tales of artists living the gringo life had altered his own Why would I go? stance, when the Palace had it all: voices, colors, drama, stories. And it wasn't that he'd changed his mind now, but that he admitted the possibility of there existing some point on the horizon that might be different from the two extremes he was bouncing back and forth between. What if . . . ? Why waste his time, he thought: one of the things he'd learned is that you stay where you're told, until you feel it's no longer your place.

He returned and knew right away there had been another tragedy, tho this time not because people rushed to the scene of the crime but because they rushed away from it, with more haste than fear, and that was truly awful. He made his way against the tide to the main courtyard. Right in the middle he saw, at first, simply a pool of blood over which the Doctor was bent, but as he approached he began to distinguish the soaking red silhouette of a man whose arms and legs were splayed, and then he recognized it as the body of the Journalist. Rage hurtled to his balled fists; this was the first time he'd lost a friend, despite never having called him that. Those motherfuckers, he said, chewing the words. The Journalist had had his throat slit clear across and was gazing up at the sky as if expecting to see someone pass. Next to his head was the flick he'd been killed with: a dagger, again, with a curved blade.

"Motherfuckers," the Artist repeated, "this time they made it all the way in."

As soon as he said it, something else popped into his head, tho he tried to push it out: I wish.

The Jeweler approached, running clumsily, looking shocked. When he got there he bent over the weapon.

The Doctor looked perplexed.

"What I don't get is what they're playing at, killing with a knife; it's grotesque."

"This wasn't the same dogs."

"How do you know?"

"This knife is different, this knife is a piece of shit."

With the speed of the subconscious, the Artist saw who shot Pocho and the Journalist and why and decided he could no longer carry on as an outside observer. He left the courtyard without a word, because now, in addition to rage, finally he felt fear. He went to find the Commoner, the Commoner, where was she? Not in her room, not in the garden, not in the corridors, not on the terrace.

"You've been with my daughter."

The Witch confronted him, suddenly there on the terrace without warning. She observed him closely, tho without the customary fury. She had made her proclamation with chilling self-possession. The Artist was amazed at how different she seemed, it was as if she'd resolved some great dilemma and were finally concerning herself with trivialities.

"Did you get her pregnant?"

The Artist instinctively said No, unable to conceive the other possibility.

"You ought to know," she continued, and held out a piece of paper on which were scribbled large, unsteady letters.

"Your girls no good to you now shes nokt up ask the singer," the note said. The Artist couldn't help but be touched when he saw the penmanship: he'd been the one to teach the Girl to trace letters and now he wondered why she would lie. Only afterward, all at once, was he

struck by the possibility that it was true, and then he
got vertigo. The note trembled in his hands. The Witch
took it and stroked the Artist's face.

"It's okay, just keep this quiet and we'll take care of it."

She gazed at him with a tenderness he recognized
but couldn't place, then turned and walked out.

He ran to the Girl's room simply to confirm that the
only traces of her were a couple of left-behind dresses.
Then, frantic, he set out once more through the Palace
in search of the Commoner, his urgency increasing with
each empty room. Not only did he know what the Witch
was capable of, he also felt the need to prevent anything
more from happening.

He found her in the games room. She was playing
solitaire at a card table, and when he walked in she
hardly even glanced up, absent.

"Is it true?" he asked.

She seemed to startle and wrinkled her forehead.
What?

Of course not. No. It couldn't be true. Or at least the
Girl couldn't have known. But the seed was already
planted and the solution began to take shape. He pulled
the Commoner gently up by the arm. Without much
conviction, she tried to shake him off.

"What's wrong? What do you want?"

"Nothing," the Artist replied. "Just let me show you
someplace."

The Artist led her from the Palace and she put up no fight nor showed any enthusiasm. He took her to a hotel far from the street, by the bridge, and told her he'd be back for her tomorrow, to wait for him. On his way out, a smell on the street made him recall which kind of tenderness the Witch had shown: he'd seen the way people pet lambs before a sacrifice.

When, the next day, he was told that the King was waiting in the library, the Artist got an inkling: he was about
to be let in on a secret; electrified, he intuited that the
relationship between them had entered new territory, a
tighter place, where they shared a more complete view
of the world that allowed mirrors like the one the Artist
had constructed to be exchanged.

"He's already been told about your latest song," said
the Manager, but the Artist was unable to read his face
and see if he'd liked it or not. He now got an inkling,
intuited a reprimand from the King, but then dismissed
it, because once he told him what he'd seen at the party
it would prove he was still on his side. The Artist even
brought his accordion along so that afterward he could
play him the song already circulating throughout the
slums, in person.

The King was bent over the wooden table, palms on
several outspread papers. He appeared not to be reading any of them, looked at them as tho searching for

something specific, or measuring them. It seemed to the Artist as if his arms were the only still-strong thing about the King, as if the rest of his body were sinking into the floor with the force of its own gravity. The Artist upsidedown read one of the papers' headlines. "The Net Tightens", it said, with a photo of the King.

He had to tell him about the party, and wanted to sing him his song, but before he articulated anything at all the King lifted his gaze and said:

"So I'm a no-account fool? That's what you say? That I can't . . . "

He fell silent. The unfinished sentence and the fact that for the first time he'd addressed him not as usted but as tú suggested, yes, that there was some new bond between them, but not the one the Artist had hoped for.

"To get where I am, it's not enough to be a badass, right. You have to *be* one and you have to *look* like one. And I am, fuck knows I am," he paused, the Artist felt the King's voice teeter between wracking sob and fit of rage, "but I need my people to believe it, and *that*, you little shit, is your job. Not running around claiming that I . . . "

His body shook as tho every bone were dying to high-tail it out of there.

"Señor, I thought . . . "

"Where the fuck did you get the idea that you could think? Where? You're a piece of fluff, a fucking music box, a thing that gets smashed, you piece of shit."

He took two steps toward the Artist, snatched his accordion, hurled it against one of the empty bookshelves and then kicked until keys and springs were scattered all over the room. His back to the Artist, fists clenched, he said:

"Still, it's my fault; that's what I get for playing with strays that bite."

The Artist knew that, following this, the King would turn and shred him, and knew that he would have the guts neither to make a stand nor to flee.

The Manager appeared all at once, almost between them, and announced:

"Señor, they're here."

The King glanced at the door to the boardroom, where a handful of green uniforms with yellow stars were taking a seat; he inhaled deeply, smoothed his hair gracelessly and walked to the room with the most timid steps the Artist had seen him take. The enemy, one of the enemies, was there, on his turf, and Señor was in anguish as if those men were of his ilk, or *as if they were the ones in charge*. The Manager closed the door behind him. The Artist heard the scraping of chairs and of the King, repeating: General, General, and then saying:

"We'll find a way around this, you'll see."

And then, nothing; but it was a condensed kind of nothing, one with texture, a nothing in which the Artist discerned an unsatisfied pause from the King, as if he couldn't carry on until he'd settled. He heard him call one of his guards, heard the guard's steps approach the head of the rectangular table and then sensed an even more informative nothing. In the time between the guard's final step and his Yessir, there was just enough time for the King to condemn him. Go jack the fucker up, he said to his soldier. That was what that nothing sounded like. Maybe the Artist could guess his words or maybe it was nothing but a surge of adrenalin that set his intuition on edge, but he lifted his feet from the floor and was off like a shot the instant the door handle began to turn, headed who knew where, with a determination he didn't know he had.

He bolted down hallways and through rooms that passed swiftly before his eyes because the Artist could hear the footsteps, clack, clack, clack of the goon behind him and urged his legs on with no sense of direction, or with some unfathomable compass that led him without warning to a blindspot. The balcony. The balcony and what lay beyond: the abyss of the desert. Or: the room that was not to be entered. Clack, clack, clack, clack comes the goon. He gripped the handle knowing that there was no hope, but the handle turned. He entered the room, stood at the center, stared at walls covered with paintings of women whose eyes seemed to follow whoever looked their way; all of them, the nude, the seated, the reclining, and those standing stiff. The Artist had seen the King enter and not exit before, knew there had to be a passageway. He quickly scanned the room and found, behind a full-length portrait, a crack, a vertical black line. Someone must have slipped out for a second and left the room unlocked. Clack, clack, clack, he heard the soldier almost outside. The Artist moved the painting: there really was a door. He slipped through and shut it behind himself, black-tar darkness flooding the space. Feeling along the walls he discovered he was in a tunnel, his stumbling feet told him he was descending short, broad steps. As he advanced, a tenuous orange glow began to light his way. The glow became a glare and the Artist arrived in another room in which he found candles in every corner, an altar, necklaces of maguey thorns, crowns of peyote, blue feathers with bloody tips, a portrait of the Holy Bandit, stones on the floor in the outline of a man, earthenware jugs overflowing with water. He slowly raised his hands, as tho afraid to shatter the image. Then he heard footsteps descending, but not the boots of his pursuer, these steps were lighter and not as swift.

And there appeared the Witch. She stopped at the end of the room with a candle in each hand. Then, staring at the Artist all the while, *acknowledging* him all the while, she stepped up to the altar.

"Have you seen my daughter?" she asked.

"She's gone."

"Is she pregnant?"

The Artist shook his head. The Witch lowered her gaze, pensive; she seemed first disappointed, then simply resigned. She placed the candles on the altar, scanning it carefully, and then looked around as tho she'd lost something.

"Who would have thought such a sorry-ass stray could fuck everything up so royally. Fine mess you made. Not only do you not help me with the baby but you tell the whole world he'll never have a child. That was all it took for them to eat him alive." And then, as if speaking to herself, she added, "If only you hadn't let my daughter get away, that other bastard might've been interested, now that he can stop pretending he's not a threat and think about his own lineage."

Suddenly the Witch lost the thread that had been holding her together: the Artist glimpsed her endless exhaustion, a fatigue he'd have thought impossible. Sadly, she asked:

"Do you know where she went?"

"No."

"Well, good luck to her, maybe she'll find an easier path." She straightened her shoulders, pulled herself together and said, "But the rest of us have still got to live here."

She left. Moments later, the Artist followed. He stepped quietly, crouched on reaching the exit tho it wasn't necessary: the Palace was deserted. Magnificent and glacial as a royal tomb. He decided to escape through a back garden, but when he was on his way out bumped smack into the Jeweler, who held a curved-blade dagger in one hand, identical, of course, to that of the first murder. Blood dripped onto the white marble.

"It was no use," the Jeweler said through his tears, "no one helped him. Now what are we going to do?"

The Artist wished that the man was not carrying a knife, not because he thought the Jeweler might hurt him but because he held it as tho it were all he had left. The Artist sensed that if he attempted to help, he'd end up in the same state. He stepped cautiously to the side to pass the knife-wielding ghost of a man and went out to the grounds.

Tho he almost tripped over the body, he hardly registered the lifeless peacock, its throat slit, as he left.

It was because he now sensed he had all the time in the world that he didn't hurl his anxieties onto the Commoner, but also because since arriving at the hotel he'd been lost, for hours, in the contemplation of the new splendor she possessed. She said nothing, the Commoner, just smiled with newborn serenity, and her body, her entire body, breathed pure, from within an aura that the Artist was afraid to defile. Like a blossom, a thing different from whatever it was he was, generating her own energy, lifeblood. Amazing, he thought; women are something else, and all you have to do is get over yourself to see how they shine.

A miracle, he felt, that a woman like her could be contemplated for hours and hours by someone like him. That was what was called a miracle. Miracle, he murmured, and was tormented by the sense that something was wrong, a chorus repeating: what gave him the right, he was taking something that wasn't his, something intended for the one who'd helped him. The notion almost broke him for a moment but then something exploded inside and brought to his lips the word No: No, he cannot rule my life. No, I will not let them tell me what to do. It was a truth he knew already, deep down, though he'd been unable to name it. The revelation made him drop to the bed. He sat there quite some time, feeling the space around him expand, and feeling with each heartbeat how the Commoner could fill it.

In the middle of the night the Artist crept out of the room. He walked to the cantina where he'd first met the King, a port like any other: lots of people passing through and a handful of faithful standbys to keep it afloat. Always the walls were dripping with dark sweat, cigarette butts lost in the sawdust like grass. The only things that looked new were the streamers, at night there were always paper streamers, and music all day, except during the brief torpor that fell when the sun was vertical. Between songs he took in the banter of the B girls and admired the customers, who could be told apart from the simple drunks by their civility: May I? And he heard the fortunes and tragedies of the average jack:

The wetback who'd been deported by immigration and was unwanted on this side as well. They'd told him to sing the anthem, explain what a molcajete was and recite the ingredients of pipián to see if he was really allowed to stay; his jitters made him forget it all so they kicked him out too. The narco-in-training who sent bindles of smack over the river with a slingshot and then simply crossed over to pick them up, until one day he got a wild hair and hit a gringo in the head with his whiterock crackshot, and tho that was the end of his business, he still got a kick out of calling himself an avenger. The woman who, to free herself of her cheating husband, sold the house to a much-feared loanshark and left hubby with no house, no wife, and no peace. The boy who faked his own kidnapping to wheedle money from his parents, who believed the ransom note was real and replied, You know what? We're tired of that bum, how about bumping him off for half the price? And the boy, out of utter sorrow, said Okay, collected the cash, spent it on booze and then kept his word.

Who was the King? An allpowerful. A ray of light who had lit up the margins because it couldn't be any other way as long as it wasn't revealed what he was. A sad sack, a man betrayed. A single drop in the sea of men with stories. A man with no power over the terse fabric inside the artist's head. (The Artist allowed himself to feel the power of an order different from that of the Court, the skill with which he detached words from things and created his own sovereign texture and volume. A separate reality.)

To say homeboy, daydream, decanter, meadowland,
rhythm. To say anything.
To listen to the sum of every silence.
To give a name to the space full of promise.
And then to fall silent.

It was all a matter of adding one plus one, stacking one stone on top of another to answer all the questions. He could have done it, and explained the whole thing to everyone, but this seemed so tedious, and he realized that he had absolutely no interest in exposing the intrigue – simply a series of incidentals exemplifying a system he now saw through.

That was what the Artist thought as he looked at a newspaper, one brought in by a new arrival who'd come at first light: there were two photos on the front page: in one, the Witch's body, peppered with countless bullet holes, dumped in with the Traitor's body, a shot to the back of the head. In the other, the King surrounded by five self-satisfied soldiers. It shook him to know the private realities behind the pictures. The vehemence that the Witch's inert body could never again express. The hidden imbroglios behind the fallen man. And there was something strange in the King's face, strange because it was out of place: he radiated satisfaction, the vanity

98

of untouched grandeur. How did he do it? The Artist read in the caption at the bottom of the photo that the King had been captured during "an intimate encounter" with three women. Right, he thought. There's a story to be sung, not the role the King had played with grace until the end, but the other tale, the one about masks, and egotism, and misery. And then he said to himself: A story for someone else to sing. Why should he refute the paper's cock and bull? At this stage he preferred the truth over the true story.

A sudden silence at the Port made him scan the tables and couples to discover what was going on. What he saw at the entrance startled him not because it was a surprise but precisely because it was so logical: it had to happen, and it hadn't occurred to him. Here came the Manager, flanked by two guards. The elegance of the former and stiffness of the latter were not only out of place in the cantina but asserted a supremacy that the crowd sensed in an instant. The Artist decided to let them come up and kill him and, more than fear, felt sadness at no longer being able to undertake all the things that in the past few hours he had glimpsed. The Manager stopped in front of him, looked over at the band and ordered: Keep playing. Gently he pushed the Artist by the forearm to one end of the bar.

"Why so far from your friends, Artist?"

"These are my friends."

With scorn the Manager eyed the couples and musicians the Artist had motioned toward.

"Cut the shit." He pointed to the Traitor's photo in the paper. "That happened to him cause he was a spent cartridge, but you're still useful. Señor wants you to come work for him."

"Señor . . . ? Who . . . ?"

"Who do you think? The man it was always meant to be."

The Artist considered it for a second and realized immediately that even if he accepted, he could never write anything to sing the Heir's praises; he seemed a man whose soul was too puckered, and the Artist no longer had eyes for people like that. If this was it, if this was his last song, so be it, at least he'd figured out a few things out before it was all over.

"I hope you'll forgive me, Manager, but I can't give what I haven't got. I'm no good for what your Señor wants, so if there's nothing else, I think I'll go my own way."

The Manager's eyes bored into him, searching for sincerity. Then he turned back to look at the Port, made a face like he wanted to spit, and he spat. It was what everyone did, but the Manager's spit had airs.

"Fine," he said then. "Your loss. Because God knows things are going to run smooth now that we're all on the same side."

He gazed at the Artist one last time, hoping, perhaps, that he'd change his mind, and then headed for the door. Before walking out, he said something to one of the guards. The guard came back to the bar, opened his jacket with one hand and let the Artist see the piece between his belly and his belt; but rather than reach for it, his hand dipped into a pocket, pulled out a bill and slipped it to the Artist.

"This is good for one thing. Get on a bus and don't come back."

The Artist watched the last guard leave and sensed that the swinging of the doors carved a final notch on his wall too. From here on out, no king named his months.

The morning sun's glare knifed his eyes the second he stepped out of the cantina and his head began pounding once more.

Back at the hotel, She was sitting on the sheets, back to the light. Staring at her own motionless shadow. Lobo watched her from the halflight. Calm. A gentle rhythm about her. But also an uneasiness that traced a hint of sorrow on her lips. And what could he tell her? Not to worry, that it would all be all right? No, but how to tell her what he knew? Mentally he stammered out a few slick sentences and realized that was no way to deliver terrible news. Lobo crossed the room and stood beside her.

"Your mother is dead."

She stared in disbelief for a second. When she realized he wasn't lying she broke into sobs and collapsed on the bed; she covered her face with her hands and wept tears of utter solitude. Lobo stroked and stroked, as if to burnish away her pain. He could do it his whole life, soothe her daybreak. Gradually, her sobbing died down and She appeared to sleep. Then all of a sudden sat up, wiped her face and said:

"We have to go, we have to get out of here."

They gathered their things and set out into the city. From one day to the next the seasons had changed and a dense, golden pollen floated in the air, but She walked quickly, as tho to flee the dust of younger days, as tho to avoid anything that might tie her down.

He waited as She bought the tickets. They ran to the bus and there, at the bottom of the steps, She stopped him:

"You can't come now," She said, "I'm not saying you should wait for me, I'm not promising anything, but you can't come now."

She gave him a long kiss, and then Lobo felt it but said nothing, he knew he couldn't stop her. He let her hand slip through his and watched her go.

Pain hammered his temples but he did not curse it. It was his. If it was death, it was his. He owned every part of himself, of his words, of the city he no longer had to find, of his love, and his patience, and the determination to return to her blood, in which, like a wellspring, he'd recognized his own.

Dear readers,

As well as relying on bookshop sales, And Other Stories relies on subscriptions from people like you for many of our books, whose stories other publishers often consider too risky to take on.

Our subscribers don't just make the books physically happen. They also help us approach booksellers, because we can demonstrate that our books already have readers and fans. And they give us the security to publish in line with our values, which are collaborative, imaginative and 'shamelessly literary'.

All of our subscribers:

- receive a first-edition copy of each of the books they subscribe to
- are thanked by name at the end of our subscriber-supported books
- receive little extras from us by way of thank you, for example: postcards created by our authors

BECOME A SUBSCRIBER, OR GIVE A SUBSCRIPTION TO A FRIEND

Visit andotherstories.org/subscribe to help make our books happen. You can subscribe to books we're in the process of making. To purchase books we have already published, we urge you to support your local or favourite bookshop and order directly from them – the often unsung heroes of publishing.

OTHER WAYS TO GET INVOLVED

If you'd like to know about upcoming events and reading groups (our foreign-language reading groups help us choose books to publish, for example) you can:

- join the mailing list at: andotherstories.org/join-us
- follow us on Twitter: @andothertweets
- join us on Facebook: facebook.com/AndOtherStoriesBooks
- follow our blog: andotherstoriespublishing.tumblr.com

Current & Upcoming Books

Born in Actopan, Mexico, in 1970, YURI HERRERA studied Politics in Mexico, Creative Writing in El Paso and took his PhD in literature at Berkeley. His first novel to appear in English, *Signs Preceding the End of the World*, won the 2016 Best Translated Book Award after publishing to great critical acclaim in 2015, when it featured on many Best-of-Year lists, including *The Guardian*'s Best Fiction and NBC News's Ten Great Latino Books. His second novel *The Transmigration of Bodies* was published in 2016 to further acclaim. He is currently teaching at the University of Tulane, in New Orleans.

LISA DILLMAN teaches in the Department of Spanish and Portuguese at Emory University in Atlanta, Georgia. She has translated a number of Spanish and Latin American writers. Some of her recent translations include *Rain Over Madrid* and *Such Small Hands* by Andrés Barba, and Yuri Herrera's three novels.